JAKE MADDOX
GRAPHIC NOVELS

VIDEO GAME VICTORS

STONE ARCH BOOKS
a capstone imprint

JAKE MADDOX
GRAPHIC NOVELS

Published by Stone Arch Books,
an imprint of Capstone.
1710 Roe Crest Drive
North Mankato, Minnesota 56003
capstonepub.com

Library in Congress Cataloging-in-Publication Data
Names: Maddox, Jake, author. | Mauleon, Daniel, 1991– authors. | Muniz, Berenice, artist.
Title: Video game victors / Jake Maddox ; text by Daniel Mauleon; art by Berenice Muniz.
Description: North Mankato, Minnesota : Stone Arch Books, | Series: Jake Maddox graphic novels | Audience: Ages 8-11 | Audience: Grades 2-3
Summary: When a local esports team asks Valentina to join them for an upcoming tournament she realizes she needs to learn teamwork to succeed.
Identifiers: LCCN 2021030692 (print) | LCCN 2021030693 (ebook) | ISBN 9781663959140 (hardcover) | ISBN 9781666328714 (paperback) | ISBN 9781666328721 (pdf) | ISBN 9781666328745 (kindle edition)
Subjects: Classification: LCC PZ7.7.M332 Vi 2022 (print) | LCC PZ7.7.M332 (ebook) | DDC 741.5/973--dc23
LC record available at https://lccn.loc.gov/2021030692
LC ebook record available at https://lccn.loc.gov/2021030693

Editor: Aaron Sautter
Designer: Brann Garvey
Production Specialist: Laura Manthe

Printed and bound in the USA. PO4608

VIDEO GAME VICTORS

Text by Daniel Mauleón
Art by Berenice Muñiz
Lettering by Jaymes Reed

CHOOSE YOUR CHARACTER

DARK ELF
SPARTAN
SPELLCASTER
ROGUE
ARCHER
VALKYRIE
KNIGHT
ORC
WARRIOR CAT
BABY DRAGON
VIKING
WIZARD
HEALER
DANCER
MAGE
PRINCESS

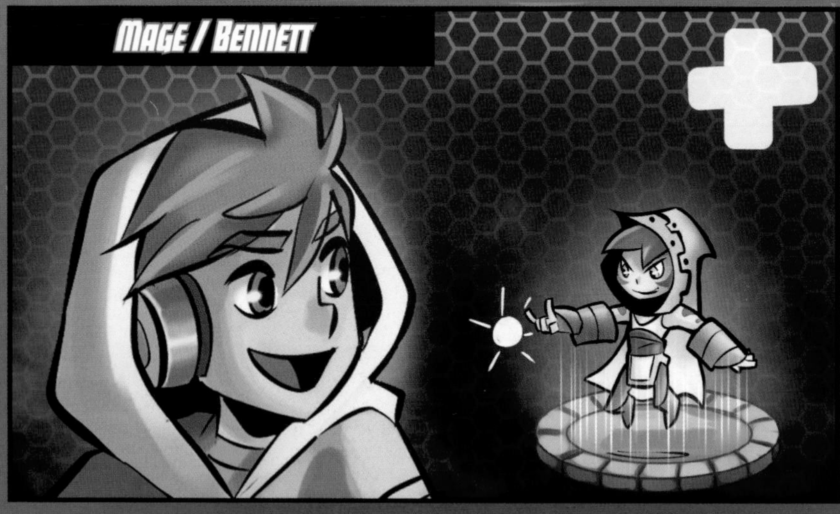

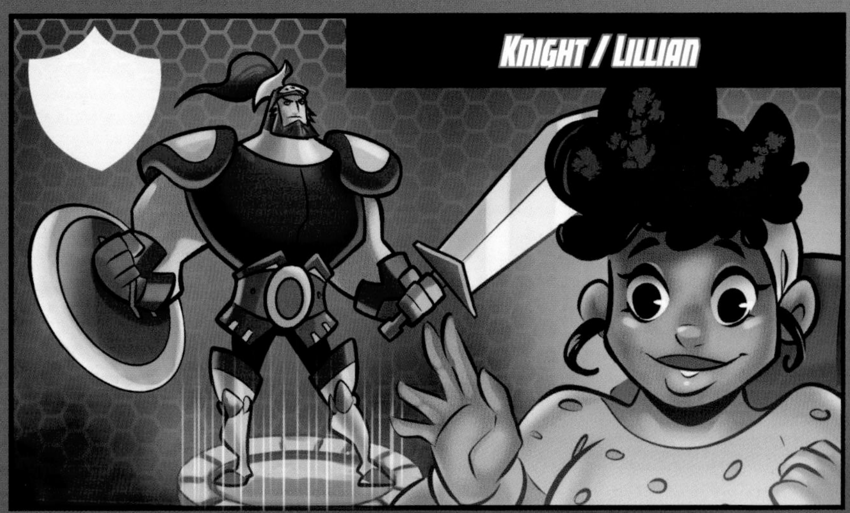
KNIGHT / LILLIAN

ARCHER / AUSTIN

BABY DRAGON / JEDIDIAH

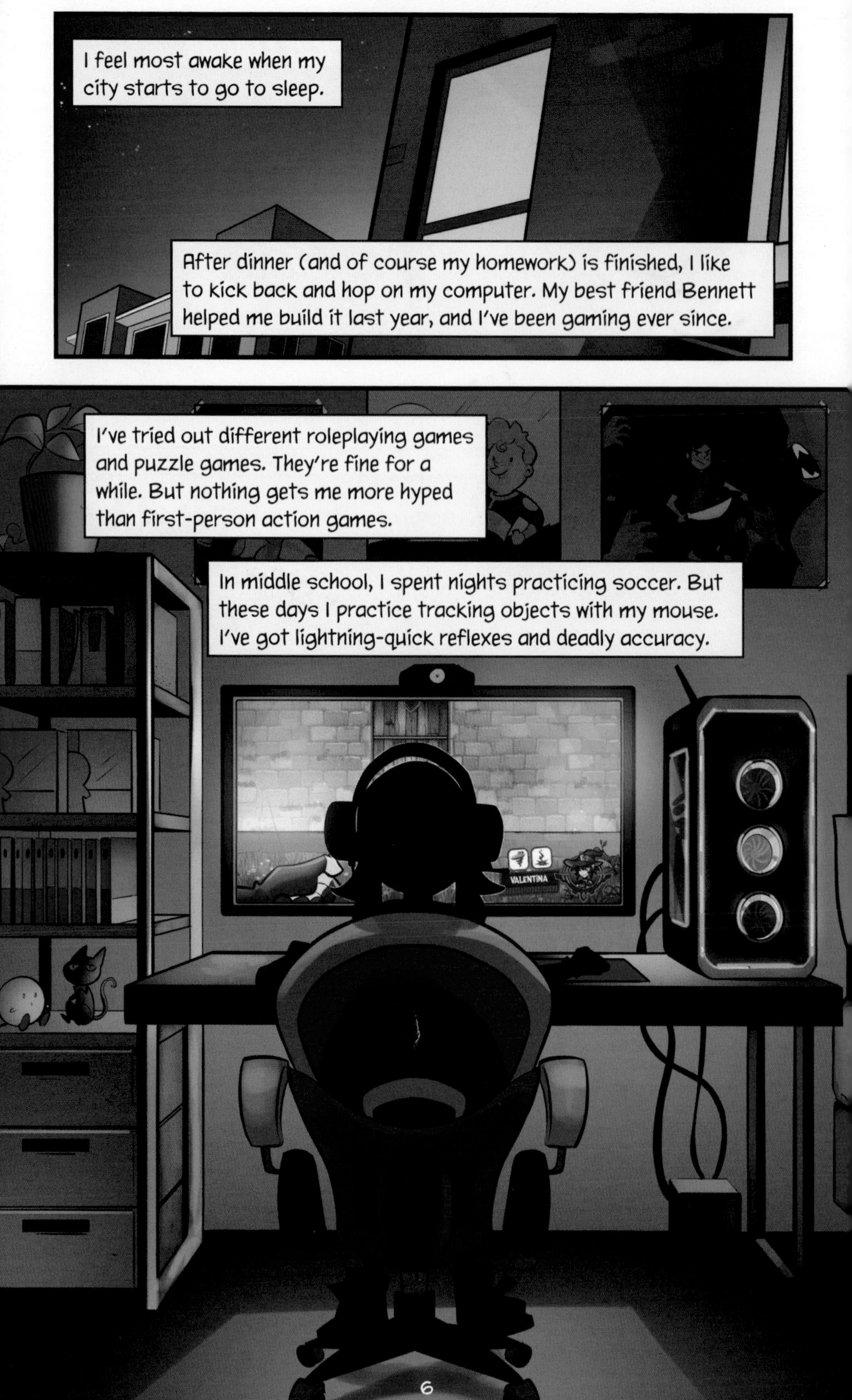

I feel most awake when my city starts to go to sleep.
After dinner (and of course my homework) is finished, I like to kick back and hop on my computer. My best friend Bennett helped me build it last year, and I've been gaming ever since.
I've tried out different roleplaying games and puzzle games. They're fine for a while. But nothing gets me more hyped than first-person action games.
In middle school, I spent nights practicing soccer. But these days I practice tracking objects with my mouse. I've got lightning-quick reflexes and deadly accuracy.
VALENTINA

I've made great progress climbing the leaderboards in several action games. But tonight . . .
. . . I'm trying out something new. It's a fantasy game called *Kings N' Castles.*
Bennett plays on a *KnC* team at school, and they need a player for a tournament this month. He knows I'm a quick learner. I figured, why not give it a shot?

TAP!

A quick tap of the space bar and my Spellcaster hops as expected. Like I said, it's pretty familiar.

The jump alone isn't enough to get across the moat. So I activate the Spellcaster's whirlwind jump.
WHOOSH!
I get across the water easily enough. But I'm not here to play a platforming game. I'm in it for the battle. And I see my first foe ahead of me!
You've got this Valentina.

I don't know every character's strengths and abilities yet. But I'm guessing by the size of the knight's sword that I don't want to get hit.
WHEEEWFF!
I quickly dodge to avoid the attack. I'm guessing that the knight is only good at close quarters combat.
So I put some space between myself and the Knight.

I take aim at the Knight's weakest point and . . .
90
VALENTINA
CLICK!
CLICK! CLICK!
. . . I unleash a flurry of magic blasts to sizzle him!
Woohoo!!

BENNETT
Hey Valentina, can you hear me?
Loud and clear Bennett!
Hey everyone! I'm Valentina, thanks for inviting me to play with you.

BENNETT
This is Lillian, our team captain!
Nice to meet you, Valentina!

BENNETT
Next is Austin. He goes to a different school, but he got permission to play on our team.
AUSTIN
Bennett says you're the best.

BENNETT
And lastly, Jedidiah!
What's up, Valentina!

I've known Bennett my whole life. So I can't help but giggle when he puts up a slideshow. It's a very Bennett move.

BENNETT: Most games you're used to have characters that specialize in damage, health, and utility.

ON KINGS 'N CASTLES

DAMAGE TANK SUPPORT

BENNETT: But *KnC* uses a role system for its character types. They're Damage, Tank, and Support.

CHOOSE YOUR CHARACTER
BENNETT
There are multiple characters for each role.
DARK ELF
SPARTAN
SPELLCASTER
ROGUE
ARCHER
VALKYRIE
KNIGHT
ORC
WARRIOR CAT
BABY DRAGON
BENNETT
But I'm just going to cover the characters currently in meta.
WIZARD
HEALER
DANCER
MAGE

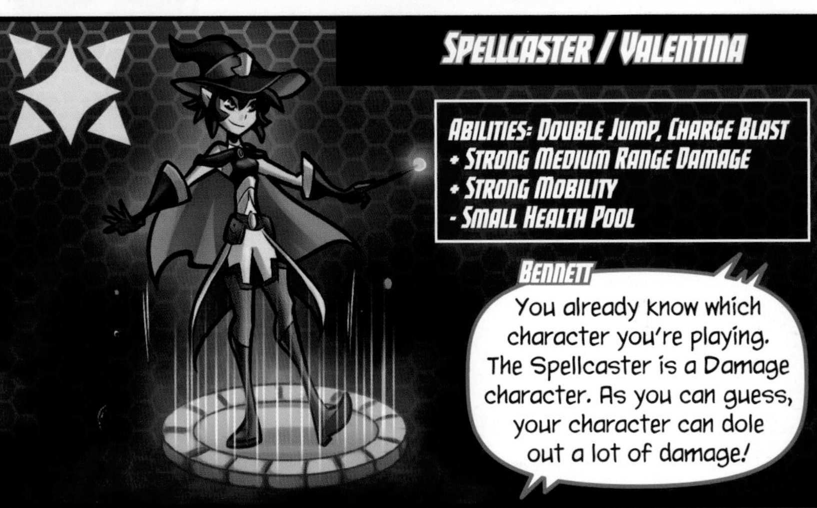
SPELLCASTER / VALENTINA
ABILITIES: DOUBLE JUMP, CHARGE BLAST
+ STRONG MEDIUM RANGE DAMAGE
+ STRONG MOBILITY
- SMALL HEALTH POOL
BENNETT
You already know which character you're playing. The Spellcaster is a Damage character. As you can guess, your character can dole out a lot of damage!

MAGE / BENNETT
ABILITIES: SHIELD CHARM, HEALING, DAMAGE BOOST
+ PROVIDES TEAM SUPPORT
- TINY HEALTH POOL
BENNETT
I play the support character, the Mage. My job is to back up the rest of the team with buffs.

KNIGHT / LILLIAN

ABILITIES: SHIELD BASH
+ LARGE HEALTH POOL
+ DEVASTATING CLOSE-RANGE DAMAGE
- SLOW MOVEMENT
- NO RANGE

BENNETT
Our fearless leader Lillian plays the equally fearless knight!

As a tank player, it's my job to take hits and make space for the rest of you!

ARCHER / AUSTIN

ABILITIES: ARCHER'S SIGHT
+ LONG RANGE ATTACKS
+ ARROWS DEAL HIGH DAMAGE
- SLOW RATE OF FIRE

BENNETT
Austin plays the second Damage character on our team.

BENNETT
There's a lot more, but this should catch you up for now.
Thanks Bennett! I appreciate all the work you put into this.
Thanks! Just let me know if you have questions.
Alright, you've got the basics. Now, about the tournament . . .

We're just two weeks away from the tournament.
We need to prepare.
We planned on playing randoms online today.
But since we have a new member, I thought we could use some real experience.
I've scheduled a scrimmage match against the Red Dragons shortly.
We'll be starting in a few minutes.
We're playing in Capture the King mode.
Valentina, if you've ever played capture the flag mode, you'll be prepared.
Gameplay generally follows this pattern . . .

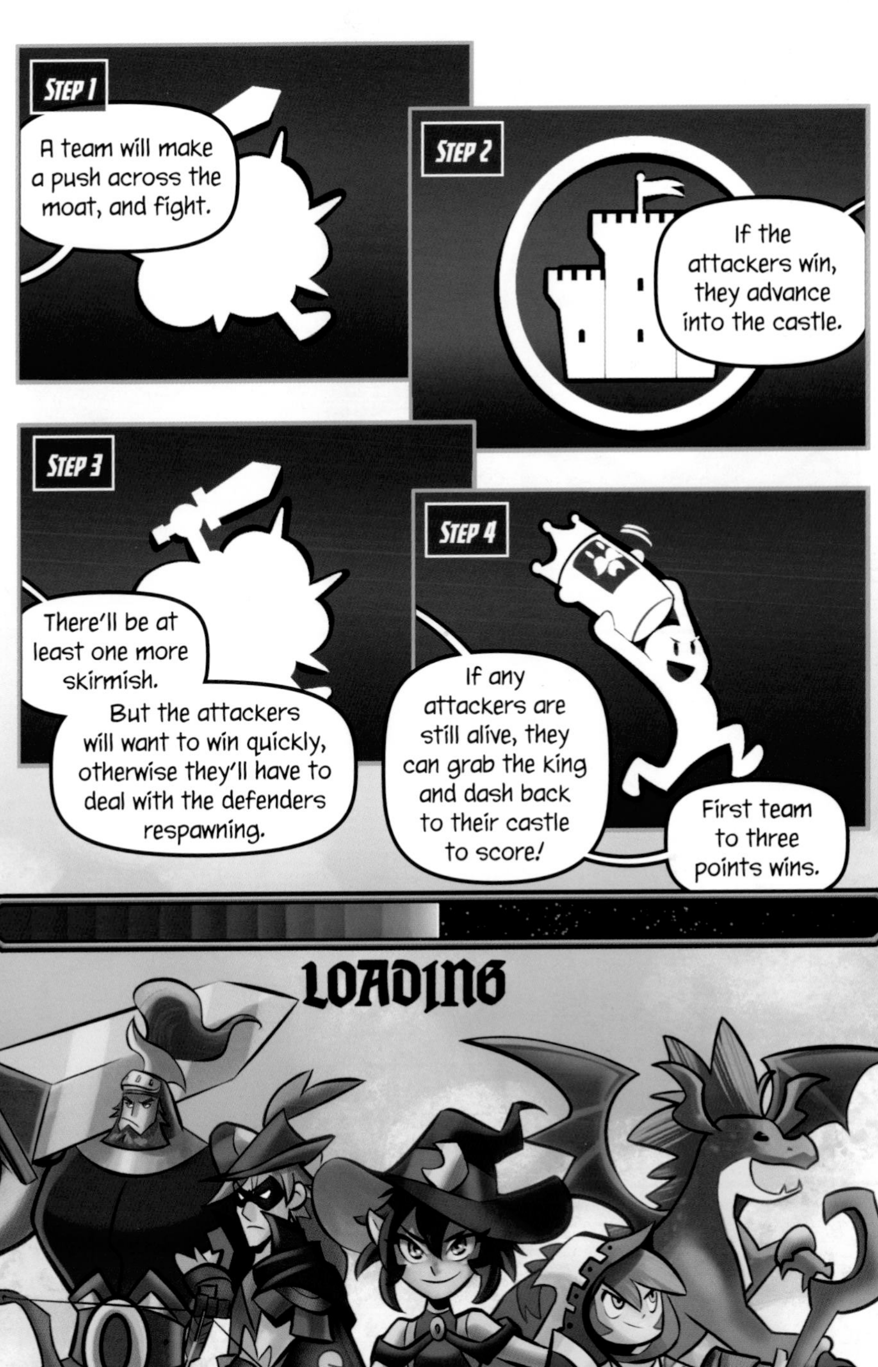
STEP 1
A team will make a push across the moat, and fight.
STEP 2
If the attackers win, they advance into the castle.
STEP 3
There'll be at least one more skirmish.
But the attackers will want to win quickly, otherwise they'll have to deal with the defenders respawning.
STEP 4
If any attackers are still alive, they can grab the king and dash back to their castle to score!
First team to three points wins.
LOADING
I got to ask a few questions, but before I knew it, we were in the game.
It was time to get my first win with the team!

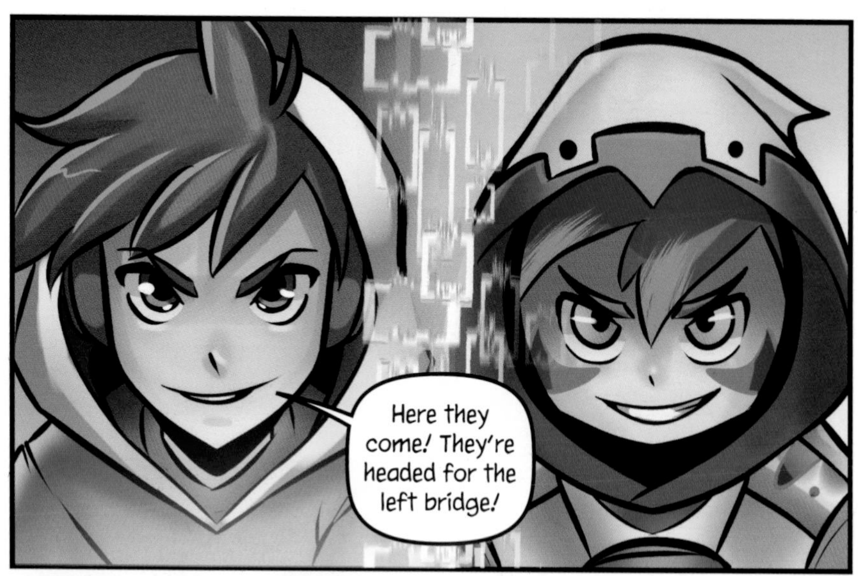
Here they come! They're headed for the left bridge!

I remember from Bennett's slide show that these are Damage characters. I should have no trouble taking them down.

I hold down the right mouse button to charge my wand and produce a powerful single shot. But I don't want to miss, and my targets are on the smaller side.

I swipe my mouse to line up the shot . . .
RED DRAGONS
ALBERT
ARMANDO
KAREN
GRACE
AUSTIN
LILLIAN
VALENTINA
SWISHH!
BLUE WOLVES
CLICK!
. . . and release the magic blast just as the cursor falls on the enemy.

zzZAP!
POOF!
One down . . .
. . . and one to go!

THUNK!
ZZZAP!
A nice combo with Austin makes quick work of the enemy Archer.
POOF!
Nice work guys! Let's go get that King!
Onward!!

Valentina, where are you going?

Don't worry about me. I've got this.

After that first fight, I'm feeling more than warmed up. I decide to take the back entrance to the throne room.

0 BLUE W

0 90 0

ARMANDO

KAREN

NEP

GRACE

VALENTINA

But first I'll have to deal with this foe. I think back to last night's game, or is that last Knight? Ha! This will be easy!

BWEEM!

Oh no! The Mage cast a Shield Charm!
P-TING!
No worries. You can still win this Valentina!
I try to back off and get some distance from the Knight. But in the small throne room it's hard to double jump.
POOF!
SWOOSH!
Before I know it, the Knight slashes me with its sword. The weapon's damage is boosted by the Mage, and I don't stand a chance.

After that, I completely lose my focus.
Every time I respawn . . .
THUNK!
. . . I get taken out by one of the enemy players.
FWOOSH!
Their Mage even takes me out!
THUNK!
It was a miserable first game. I won't be surprised if the others look for a different player.
uughhh . . .

Good game everyone. How are we feeling?

They were strong.

That was a blast!

How are you doing Valentina?

Honestly, I want to melt away in my chair. But the others aren't acting upset. So, I give it a chance.
That was bad.
I was bad. I don't even know what happened.
When I played last night, I had no trouble with any of those matchups.
But I got wrecked today.

That's not surprising.
When you play in random lobbies, even in team modes, its a free-for-all.
I'm not surprised you shined.
LILLIAN
But in scrimmages, and the upcoming tournament, it'll take the whole team to win—and not just a single player.
Lillian talks like I'm already part of the team. It helps turn my spirits around. I can see why she's captain. If she can trust me, maybe I can trust the team.
That makes sense.
If you all don't mind, could you tell me what I can do better?

I'm always willing to call out when you mess up! Ha ha!
Just kidding V.
Really, you just need to think of each matchup as an equation. If a Mage pockets a character, it means you'd better play out of your mind or call for back up.
Communication is also key. 
We have unique words for each character and location on the map.
That way we can coordinate our movements on the fly or target certain enemies.

I saw you crash and burn as the game went on.

You got tilted.

It's important to keep a cool mind.

Learn to shrug off your mistakes.

And remember to have fun.

That's great advice.

Thanks everyone!

I don't know how they do it, but I've never gotten this excited to play another game. And I'm ready to do what it takes to win.

I spend the next few days grinding in the game.
Bennett teaches me the different ways support characters can boost others.
I review VODS with Lillian.
You should keep an eye on your ability timers.
Watch here . . . see how you got into this fight before your double jump had charged up?
Jedidiah doesn't teach me anything specific. We just goof off and have fun playing together.
GRRWAAHHHH!
Did you just roar into your mic?
What? I'm a dragon! Dragons roar!

Austin taught me character callouts.
K&C NAMES
ARCHER = BOW
SPELLCASTER = WITCH
MAGE = MAGE (LOL)
DRAGON BABY = BABY
KNIGHT = KNIGHT
POWER!
ATTACK
ATTACK
ATTACK!
Quiz time! What do we call the secret throne room entrance?
"Stairwell" or "stairs" for short?
Ding, Ding, Ding!
MATH HOMEWORK
Before I knew it, it was Saturday—the day of the tournament.
GAME DAY
9:00 AM

Instead of playing from our own homes, we gathered at school to play together.

Nervous?

Never. You?

Oh . . . always.

When I see everyone getting set up, my heart starts beating faster. It turns out that I'm a bit nervous after all.

CALM AND DON'T TURN OFF THE COMPUTER

COMPUTER

RETRO GADGETS

RESPECT THE LAPTOP!

KEEP YOUR PASSWORD TO YOURSELF

Welcome you two! Let me know if you need any help setting up.

It's weird to meet someone in person for the first time, but at the same time it feels like they're already your friend.
Hey Valentina! Great to finally meet you.
You too!
Hate to interrupt, but everyone gather up.
Let's go over a few things.
As you know we're playing single elimination matches.
Matchups came out this morning.
BLUE WOLVES
GREEN ELVES
GOLD KNIGHTS
BLACK CROWS
BROWN HORSES
PURPLE GNOMES
RED DRAGONS
I think we have a great chance at getting to the finals.
There's also a good chance we'll be playing the Red Dragons there.
Okay. Now I'm a LOT nervous.

After a little while, we're all set to play. Not playing in my room feels different. My table is a bit higher here, and my monitor a bit lower.

I've been practicing non-stop.
I'll be okay. Right?

VRING!
VRING!
VRING!
I can't explain it. I'm missing every shot I take.
Ughh!
Valentina! Where are you going? Stick with us.
I completely forgot what we practiced and fell back on my old habits.

Thankfully, the others were playing well . . .
POOF!
POOF!
RUN!
What do you think I'm doing!
Jedidiah and Austin had it covered.
They captured the other team's king THREE times!
Way to go!
Thanks for the backup.
I felt like dead weight.

I started the next game thinking about how badly I was playing.

But I had to remember . . . it isn't about me. It's about working with my team.

I still missed some shots, but round two went better.
Sorry I'm not playing my best.
That's okay, you're playing with us, that's what's important.
We have each other's back.

Bennett's words are comforting. I'm feeling less nervous. However . . .
. . . if we want a shot at winning, I need to work well with my team AND play at my best.

FINAL ROUND
VS
BLUE WOLVES
RED DRAGONS

We decide to open the round playing defense. We stand guard to keep an eye on the enemy's movements.
Here they come!
Is that . . .
. . . ALL OF THEM!?
It's a bold move. The Red Team left their King undefended to launch a full-on attack. And although we were on defense . . .
VRINNG!
FFFT!
. . . we weren't ready.

Bennett!!
POOF!
Fall back!!
Fall back!!
The previous teams we faced had played so cautiously. I thought that the Red Dragons were being reckless with this attack.
FWOOSH!
When I see two of them split off, I think I have a chance to take them out. Their opening push felt chaotic to us . . .

. . . but for them, it was all part of the plan.
Oops.
THWANG!
POOF!
FWIZZ!
1 - 0
Apparently, Jedidiah and Austin had bad luck inside the throne room too. Within a minute the Red Team had captured our king and scored. And we hadn't taken out a single enemy during the fight.

Shake it off, everyone. Let's match their aggression.
Jedidiah, Valentina, and Bennett, you three make a push for their castle.
Let's gooooooo!
Jedidiah's energy is infectious.
Let me give us some cover!
I wonder if Lillian paired us up so we can rally off of Jedidiah's good vibes.

However, even though our push toward the target is feeling good . . .
. . . things fall apart.
Um, Bennett? What're you doin' down there?
Ugh. I couldn't see the edge of the bridge and fell off.
My bad everyone. I'll catch up shortly.
Things quickly go from bad to worse.
POOF!
POOF!
As we look down at Bennett, the Red Dragons' Knight sneaks up on us . . .

. . . which gives the Red Dragons another easy score.
2-0
Keep your cool everyone . . .
. . . the game isn't over yet.
We know they like to play aggressive.
We can use that.
I don't know how Lillian can be smiling when we're down by two. But she's right. This is the finals, and we've earned the right to be here.

We decide to slow things down and wait for their next approach. Sure enough, two of the red team members move in on our castle . . . where Lillian appears to be alone.
NOW!
Call your targets!
FWIZZ!
FWIZZ!
BOW-BOW-BOW-BOW!

I use the character callouts that Austin taught me. Together, Lillian and I focus on the enemy Archer first.
FWZZZ!
FWZZZ!
CLANG!
SWOOSH!
BABY-BABY-BABY!
The Archer drops immediately, but their Baby Dragon takes a few more hits.
FWZZZ!
FWZZZ!
But he's no match as the three of us work together.
POOF!
For the first time in the game we have the advantage. So we take the opportunity to storm the castle.
Good work, everyone!
Keep your eyes open!

As we enter the red castle, I look back to see the enemy Spellcaster heading toward our base.
I've been watching this player throughout the game. I could take them in a duel. But I'm part of a team.
Hey Austin, the enemy witch is coming your way.
Thanks for the heads up.
Austin knows what he has to do—and so do I.
Alright squad! Let's snag that . . .

. . . King.
This feels too familiar. I could target the Mage first. Then I could get some distance to fight the Knight. Or better yet . . .

I let Lillian take on the Red Knight while I draw my wand and fire at their Mage.
TAP!
VWEEEEEM!
CLANG!
CLICK!
CLICK! CLICK!
TAP!
ZAP!
ZAP!
ZAP!

CLICK!
CLICK! CLICK!
POOF!
POOF!
With no Mage for back up, the Red Knight falls.
We make our way back with their King and score our first point!

For the first time all day, maybe all month, I feel alive. I'm not even playing at my best. It's because I'm playing with my team.
We're down by one point and time is ticking.
We need to be bold. I'd like to make a suggestion.
Let's keep up the momentum and go in—all of us.

Works for me.
Good idea V!
Let's go!
Sounds good.
We decide to split into two parties. That way we can come at them from two sides. We don't know where the red team is in their castle, but we're ready for the fight.

When we enter the castle it's much more chaotic then I expected. I wonder how we should practice for this kind of battle in the future. It's the first time I've thought about playing with the group beyond this tournament.
ROOARR!
ZAP!
SCRSSH!
CRSSH!
CLINK!
POOF!
VWEEEEM!

During the chaos in the battle, Bennett grabs the enemy's King and runs back to our castle. The enemy team chases him the whole way. In the end, he's able to tie the game . . .
2 - 2
. . . and does it just in time.
The game runs out of time. With the score tied, it triggers sudden death mode. The kings are brought closer together, and we don't get to respawn.
BRIIING!
00:00
BRIIING!
SUDDEN DEATH

It all comes down to this.
TAP!
CLICK!
CLICK!
TAP!
Shoot! I'm out.
TAP!
Red Mage is down!
TAP!

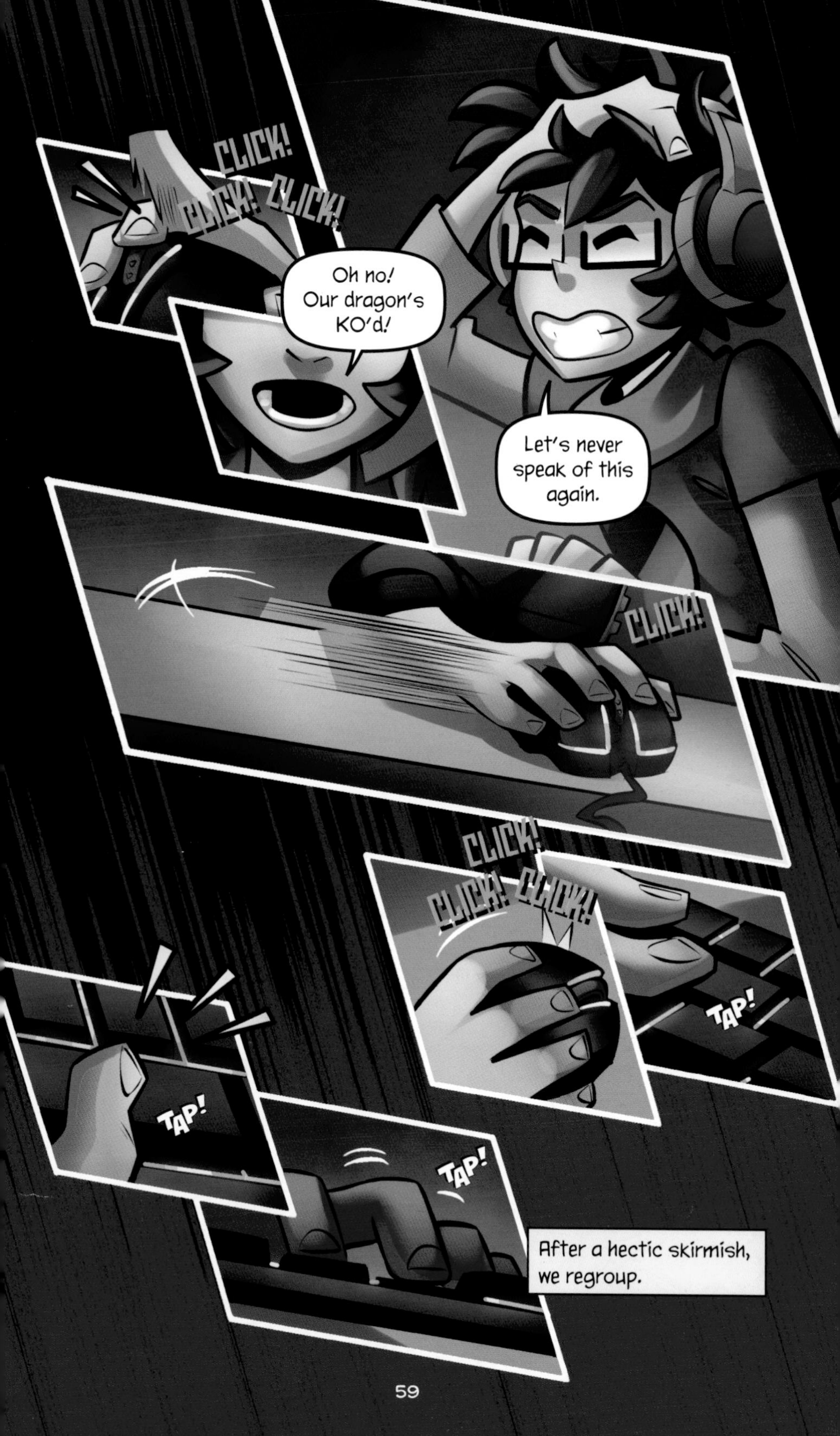
CLICK!
CLICK! CLICK!
Oh no! Our dragon's KO'd!
Let's never speak of this again.
CLICK!
CLICK!
CLICK! CLICK!
TAP!
TAP!
TAP!
After a hectic skirmish, we regroup.

We suffered some losses in the first fight . . .
. . . but so had they!

The Red Knight stands between me and the king. He's beat up, and doesn't have a Mage for support.

I've never felt more confident in a matchup. But . . .

. . . I decide to play it smart.
Hey Bennett, can I get a boost?
Happy to!

I scoop up the king and make a mad dash for our castle.
Keep going! I've got your back!
2 - 3

Thanks for playing with us!

It was a blast!

Great work today Valentina.
Thanks.
So, I was going to ask you. We have another tournament in a month.
Care to join the team officially?
Absolutely! Count me in!

VISUAL DISCUSSION QUESTIONS

1. Look at the characters above. In what ways are the story's characters similar to the characters they played in the game? In what ways are they different?

2. Look at the icon in the lower left corner of this panel. Can you tell what ability the character is using based on this symbol?

3. Graphic artists can show a lot of action in a single panel. Look at the scene to the right. Can you tell which characters are winning this intense battle?

4. The way scenes are lit can help add certain moods to a story. How does the lighting in these panels help increase the action or drama in each scene?

MORE ABOUT ESPORTS

The first major esports tournament was held in 1980. More than 10,000 players competed for the best score in *Space Invaders* for a spot in the finale in New York. Rebecca Ann Heineman won first place at just 16 years old!

Participating in high school esports can open the door to more opportunities. More than 170 U.S. colleges have esports programs with annual scholarships of more than $16 million.

The fictional game *Kings N' Castles* is based on team-based shooters such as *Team Fortress* and *Overwatch. Overwatch* has its own international league with teams from seven states and more than five countries.

When the League of Legends World Championship began in 2011, the winning team earned $50,000! The prize grew each year and peaked in 2018 at $2.4 million!

ESPORTS WORDS TO KNOW

buff—a power-up used by one player to boost another player's ability

first-person—a type of video game where players view the action through the eyes of the character they are playing

melee—low damage hand-to-hand combat performed at close range in a game; often involving handheld weapons

meta—the current set of characters or strategies that are being used by players

pocketing—when a support character is dedicated to helping another player, instead of the whole team

push—when a team moves together toward an objective

respawn—when a character reenters the game after being knocked out

skirmish—a fight between several players from both sides of a game

third-person—a type of video game where players view the action from above or behind the character they are playing

tilted—when a player is so frustrated or angry that they begin playing poorly

tracking—the ability of a player to follow targets accurately across a screen

VOD (Video-on-Demand)—recorded video of a game that players can replay to study their or their opponents' moves

GLOSSARY

advantage (ad-VAN-tij)—a condition in which a team has the edge over an opponent in a competition

close quarters combat (KLOHS KWOR-turs KOM-bat)—a fight that takes place in a small space with little room to move around

cursor (KUR-ser)—a moveable marker that indicates where a character is looking or aiming a weapon in a game

leaderboard (LEE-dur-bohrd)—a list showing the names and scores of the top players in a game

mobility (moh-BIL-uh-tee)—the ability to move quickly and easily

momentum (moh-MEN-tuhm)—a quality of a team that has confidence and is playing well together

platforming game (PLAT-form-ing GAYM)—a game in which a player controls a character to jump between levels and avoid various obstacles to achieve a goal

roleplaying game (ROHL-play-ing GAYM)—a game where players take on the roles of imaginary characters and take part in an adventure

scrimmage (SKRIM-ij)—a practice game

single elimination (SING-uhl ih-lim-uh-NAY-shuhn)—a type of tournament in which the loser of each matchup is removed from competition

tournament (TUR-nuh-muhnt)—a series of matches between several players or teams, ending in one winner